To Sarah and Sean, two of the most important people in my life
and
to Mike, for helping me realize *"the most important thing"* in such a difficult time – R.R.

To Grandma Jane for gracing me with all of her wisdom – S.G.

The Most Important Thing

RHONDA ROTH

Illustrated by SHANE GRAJCZYK

CROSSING GUARD BOOKS · CROSSING GUARD BOOKS · COLORADO

Sadie came bouncing into the living room where her parents were sitting on the couch talking.

She had been playing outside with her friends, but her happy mood vanished quickly when she noticed tears in her mother's eyes and a sad look on her father's face. She also noticed the way they stopped talking when they saw her standing there. "They don't look happy. What could they be talking about?" she wondered.

Mom turned her head and wiped away the tears.
Dad quickly smiled back, but Sadie could tell it
wasn't his happy smile. Mom asked, "How about
a hug, my angel?" Sadie ran over and gave
each of them a big hug. Then Mom
said, "Now run upstairs and play
for a while." Sadie nodded.
"Sure," she said.

Moving up the stairs very slowly, she strained to hear what they were talking about. She was only able to catch one phrase. Her mother said something about "the most important thing."

Wondering what "the most important thing" could possibly be,
Sadie finally made her way upstairs and into her bedroom at the
end of the hall. She closed her bedroom door, plopped down
hard on her bed, and hugged Teddy to her chest.

She didn't feel like playing. Her parents seemed so
unhappy lately. They didn't smile anymore. They
hardly talked to each other, and when they did it was
usually in whispers.

Sadie knew something was *wrong*.

A few weeks later Sadie was sitting in her third grade classroom when the end-of-school bell rang. Mrs. Williams, Sadie's teacher, who she liked very much, dismissed the class. She asked Sadie to stay behind. As Sadie's classmates gathered their belongings and filed slowly out the door, she saw her parents standing in the hall.

After all the other students had left the classroom,
Sadie's mother and father came in and greeted her teacher.
"Good afternoon, Mrs. Williams. It's so nice to see you again."

"Mom, Dad, what are you doing here?" asked Sadie.

Sadie was worried. She tried to remember if she'd done something wrong. Noticing the look on Sadie's face, Dad smiled and assured her, "Don't worry, sweetheart; you haven't done anything wrong."

Mom turned to Sadie and explained that they wanted to talk with Mrs. Williams. Sadie said, "But, Mom, mid-year conferences were just last month."

"Yes, I know, Sadie, and we discussed how well you are doing. But today we need to discuss another very important matter with your teacher."

Sadie was about to sit back down when Mrs. Williams asked, "Sadie, would you like to go next door and help Mrs. Peterson change her bulletin boards?"

Even though Sadie loved to help Mrs. Peterson and would normally jump at the chance, all she could think about were her mother's words: "We need to discuss another very important matter." Sadie wanted to stay and listen, but she knew Mrs. Williams wasn't really asking, and she didn't really have a choice.

As she left the room, she heard her teacher say, "the most important thing." "Hmmm, what could that be?" she wondered.

Sadie knew something was *wrong.*

The next morning Sadie woke bright and early.
"Yay! It's Saturday!" she exclaimed. "What a beautiful day!"

Pulling her favorite shirt over her head and thinking about
all the wonderful things she'd like to do, she heard the front
doorbell ring.

She finished dressing and raced
down the stairs to answer the door.
"Grandma!" she screamed.

Grandma rushed inside to greet her. "My Sadie girl! Oh, how I've missed you!" she said. "Let me see that beautiful face!" Sadie's big blue eyes lit up as she smiled. She gave her grandmother a big hug and kiss. She was very happy to see her.

Mom, Grandma, and Sadie were soon sitting at the dining room
table eating a delicious Saturday morning breakfast. Mom
explained that Dad was at the office. He had to go to work today.

Sadie noticed a strange glance shared between her mother and grandmother. She wondered what it was about.

When they had all finished eating, Mom announced, "Sadie, you can go outside and play while Grandma and I do the dishes. Then we will all go to a movie."

"Uh-oh, not this again," thought Sadie. "They are trying to get rid of me. Mom knows I like helping in the kitchen, even doing the dishes." But sensing how much her mother wanted to have a private talk with Grandma, Sadie smiled and said, "OK."

So she slid open the back door and stepped outside. Before she
closed the door, she heard her grandmother say, "the most important
thing." Again, Sadie wondered what that could mean.

She knew something was *wrong*.

A few days later Sadie was riding the bus home from a great day at
school. She had made an A on her spelling test, and the new girl in
her class wanted to be her friend.

The bus drove down Sadie's street and stopped in front
of her house. She noticed a strange black car parked
in the driveway. Wondering who could be visiting,
she ran to her house and opened the front door.

Sitting in the living room were Mom, Dad, and a strange woman in a fancy business outfit. Sadie could tell this was a very important meeting. The woman had a notepad and was taking notes.

Dad introduced them. "Sadie, this is Mrs. Lowery. She is an attorney." Then he said, "Why don't you go into the kitchen and get a snack. Mother and I will be in shortly to discuss something very important."

As Sadie walked to the kitchen, the adults continued their conversation, and she heard her father say, "the most important thing." She knew something was wrong, and she had a feeling she was about to find out what it was.

Sadie reached into the cookie jar and grabbed a few of her favorite chocolate chip cookies. She poured herself a glass of milk and sat at the table with her snack, but she couldn't eat. Her stomach was too nervous.

Soon Sadie's parents said goodbye to Mrs. Lowery and came into
the kitchen. They sat down at the table beside her. Dad began by saying,
"Sadie, your mother and I love you very much." Then Sadie heard the
words she didn't want to hear, but somehow knew were coming. Her
mother said, "Sadie, your father and I are
getting a divorce."

Sadie wanted to burst out
crying. She was so angry and
so hurt. "How could they do
this to me?" she thought.

Mom said that although this was a sad situation, it was definitely not going to be a bad one. They explained how the two of them had grown apart and wanted different things in life. But they made it very clear that it was not Sadie's fault and that they both loved Sadie very much.

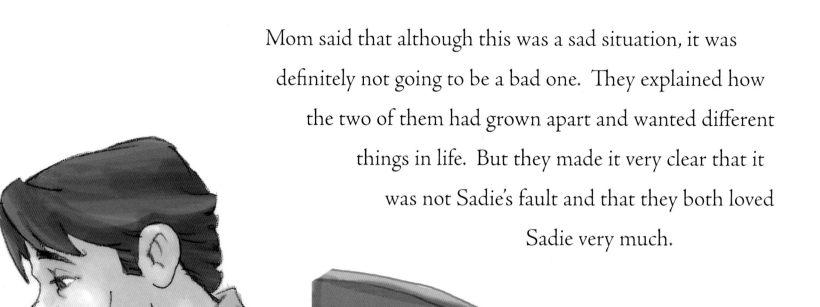

As Sadie fought back the tears, she remembered the conversations she had overheard and the phrase everyone kept repeating, "the most important thing." A look of shock came over her face, and she screamed, "So this DIVORCE is 'the most important thing' I've been hearing you talk about?"

Both of Sadie's parents, at the same time, said, "No, Sadie, YOU are the most important thing!" They said, "No matter what happens, YOU are our first concern: your happiness, your health, and your education. YOU are the most important thing to both of us!"

Sadie cried and hugged her parents for a long time. She knew she may never get used to this divorce, but she was beginning to feel a little better about it.

Sadie realized how much her parents loved her and that she really was the most important thing.

Sadie knew everything would be ok.

The most important thing you can do for a child?

Talk to them.

Text copyright © 2007 by Rhonda Roth
Illustration copyright © 2007 by Shane Grajczyk
All Rights Reserved.

Published in the United States by Crossing Guard Books, an imprint of Longs Peak Publishing, Inc.
P.O. Box 1792, Loveland, CO 80538

ISBN-13: 978-0-9770141-0-1
ISBN-10: 0-9770141-0-X
Library of Congress Control Number: 2005935968
www.CrossingGuardBooks.com
Printed in China